Lauren Child

I am TOO ABSOLUTELY small for SCHOOL

Featuring **Charlie** and **Lola**

for Sofie and her
invisible friend
Søren Lorensen

and for Maisie, Clemmie,
Molly and Ella

This edition published in 2015

ISBN 978 1 84616 885 7

First published in 2003 by Orchard Books

Absolutely thank you to Goldy for taking all the photographs so beautifully

ORCHARD BOOKS Carmelite House 50 Victoria Embankment

London EC4Y 0DZ

8 10 9 7

The right of Lauren Child to be identified as the author and illustrator of this book

© Lauren Child 2003 & 2015 Text and illustrations

her work has been asserted by her in accordance with the Copyright, Designs and Patents Act, 1988.

Thank you to Simon for his utterly invaluable comments

A CIP catalogue record for this book is available from the British Library.

An imprint of Hachette Children's Group

Orchard Books Printed in China

Part of The Watts Publishing Group Limited An Hachette UK Company

www.hachette.co.uk

I have this little sister Lola. She is small and very funny.

Now Mum and Dad say she is nearly quite big enough to go to school.

Lola is not so sure.

Charlie

huge

giantish

big

biggish

smallish

Slightly small

small

tiny

teeny

titchy

Lola

says,

"I am **absolutely** not **BIG.**

I am still

really quite small."

She says,

"I probably do not have time to go to school. I am too extremely busy doing important things at home."

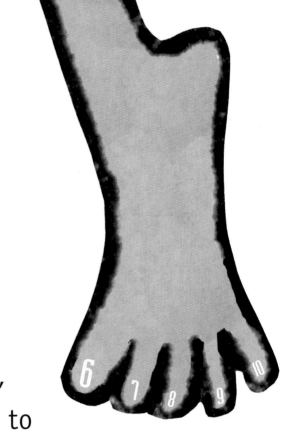

I say,
"At school
you will learn
numbers and how to
count up to one hundred."

Lola says,
"I don't need to
learn up to one hundred.
I already know up to ten
and that is plenty.

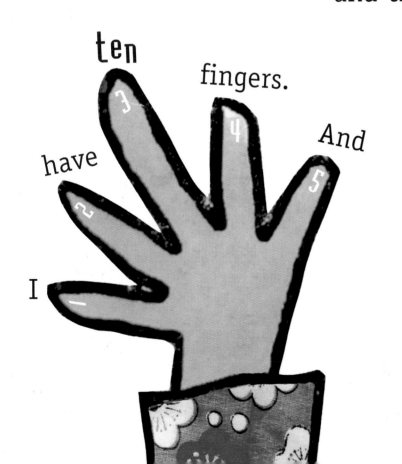

ten

fingers.

have

And

I

also

I have

ten

toes.

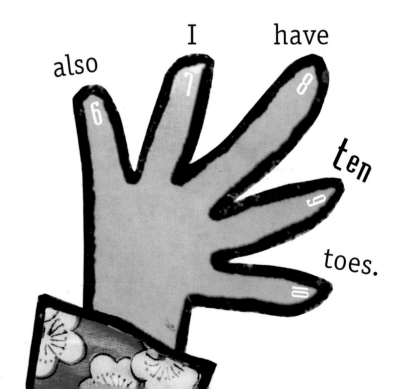

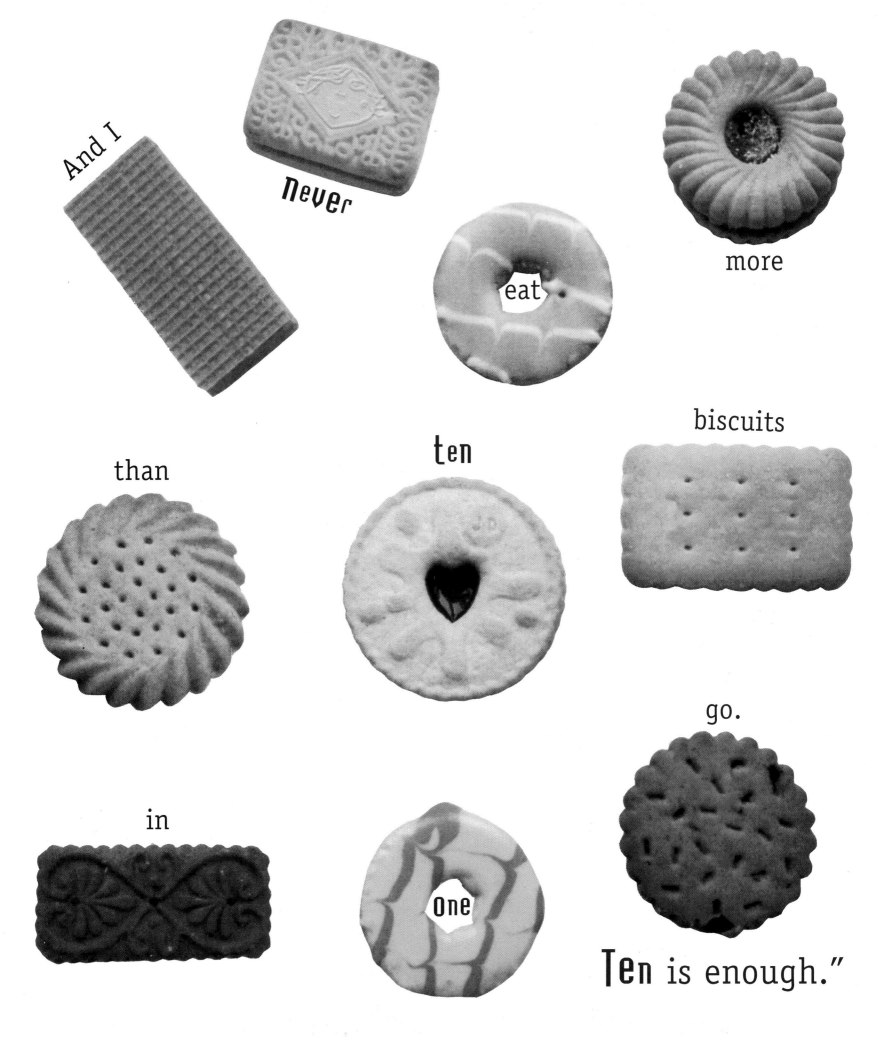

And I

Never

more

eat

than

ten

biscuits

in

One

go.

Ten is enough."

How would you count up how many treats that would be?"

"Well," says Lola.

"I am not quite sure."

I say,

"And what about learning your

letters, Lola?

If you know how to write,

you can send cards to

people you like."

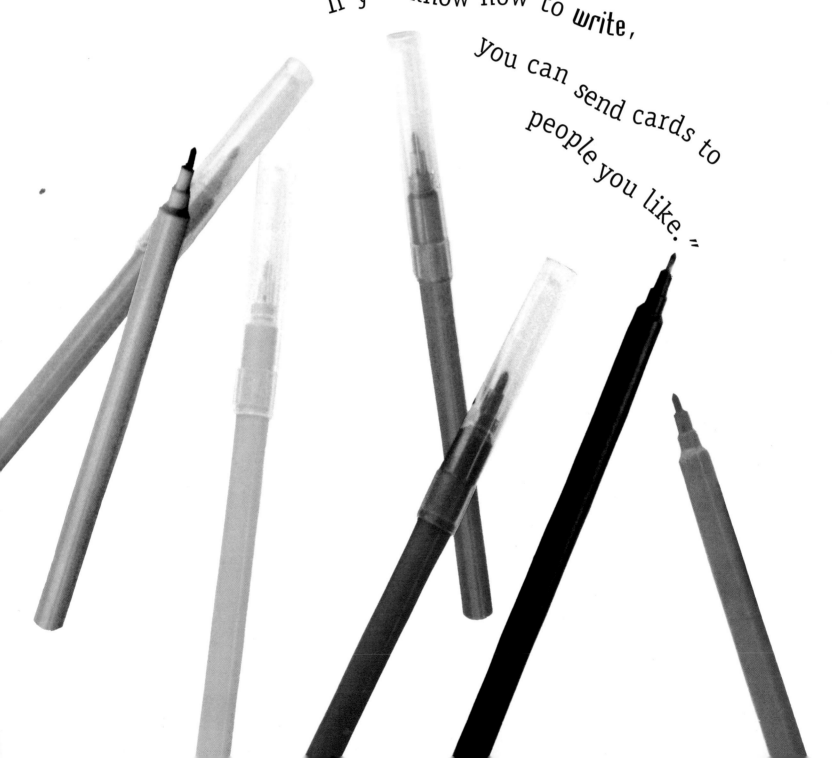

"But not everyone has a telephone you know,

Lola," I say.

"Who doesn't?" says Lola.

"Father Christmas," I say. "You have to write him a special note and put it up the chimney to tell his little helpers your Christmas wish. Otherwise the little helpers might get your wish muddled up."

"I didn't know that, Charlie," says Lola.

"And Lola," I say,
    "don't you want to
read words? Then you will
        be able to **read** your
own **books**. And understand
secret messages written
on the fridge."

Lola says,
    "I know lots of **secrets**.
I don't need to **read words**,
        and I've got all my
books in my head.
        If I can't remember, I
can just make them up."

"But Lola," I say, "what would you do if there was an ever so angry ogre who would not go to sleep unless you read him his favourite bedtime story?"

"I don't know, Charlie,"

says Lola.

Then Lola says,
     "I would like to
read to an ogre and
     count up elephants and
put notes up the chimbley.
But I absolutely will NOT
     ever wear a schooliform.
I do not like wearing the
same as other people."

I say,
     "But Lola, you do
not have to wear a
     school uniform. At our
school you can wear
          whatever you like."

"Oh," says Lola.
     "You wait there. I know
exactly what I can wear..."

"Well, Lola," I say, "that certainly suits you,

but you **cannot** go to school dressed as a **crocodile**."

Lola says, "This is **not** a **crocodile**, this is a **alligator**."

I say, "You can't really go as an **alligator** either."

"Why not?" says Lola.

charlie

My sister Lola is fussy about food.

"But Lola, you can take your very own packed lunch in your very own lunch box."

I say,

You know I will NOT ever never eat a school dinner."

"I like to wear stripes," says Lola, "but what will I do at lunchtime?

Lola says, "I do not want to eat at school, **alone**, all by myself on my own."

Lola

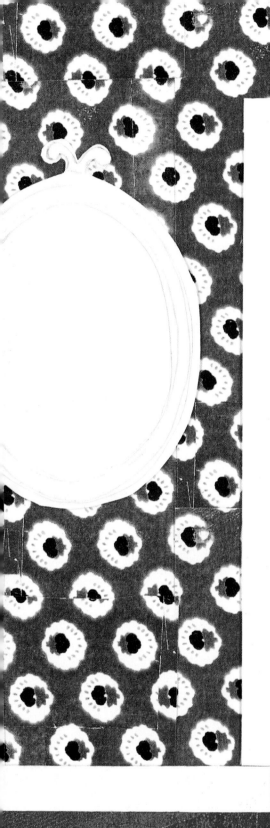

I say, "But Lola, at school you will meet lots of new **friends**. You can have **lunch** with one of them."

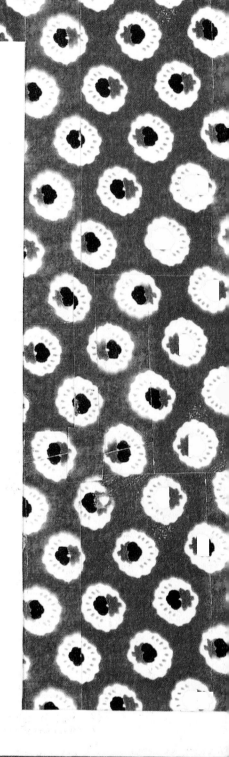

Then Lola says, "But I already have **my friend** Soren Lorensen. I would like to have **lunch** at **home** with him."

Soren Lorensen is Lola's invisible friend. No one knows what he looks like.

Walking to school, Lola is all wobbly.

She says, "Soren Lorensen is feeling slightly not very well.

He is worried he will not be able to count numbers, do letters and read words, and no one will

"Lola," I say, "it will be OK.

You'll be fine.

I bet you'll both have a really good time.

And after school we'll have pink milk at home."

talk to him so he will be all by himself on his own."